Dear Parents:

Congratulations! Your child is taking
the first steps on an exciting journey.
The destination? Independent reading!

STEP INTO READING® will help your child get there. The program offers
five steps to reading success. Each step includes fun stories and colorful
art or photographs. In addition to original fiction and books with favorite
characters, there are Step into Reading Non-Fiction Readers, Phonics Readers
and Boxed Sets, Sticker Readers, and Comic Readers—a complete literacy
program with something to interest every child.

Learning to Read, Step by Step!

Ready to Read   Preschool–Kindergarten
• big type and easy words • rhyme and rhythm • picture clues
For children who know the alphabet and are eager to
begin reading.

Reading with Help   Preschool–Grade 1
• basic vocabulary • short sentences • simple stories
For children who recognize familiar words and sound out
new words with help.

Reading on Your Own   Grades 1–3
• engaging characters • easy-to-follow plots • popular topics
For children who are ready to read on their own.

Reading Paragraphs   Grades 2–3
• challenging vocabulary • short paragraphs • exciting stories
For newly independent readers who read simple sentences
with confidence.

Ready for Chapters   Grades 2–4
• chapters • longer paragraphs • full-color art
For children who want to take the plunge into chapter books
but still like colorful pictures.

STEP INTO READING® is designed to give every child a successful
reading experience. The grade levels are only guides; children will progress
through the steps at their own speed, developing confidence in their reading.
The F&P Text Level on the back cover serves as another tool to help you
choose the right book for your child.

Remember, a lifetime love of reading starts with a single step!

Visit us on the Web!
StepIntoReading.com
rhcbooks.com

Educators and librarians, for a variety of teaching tools, visit us at
RHTeachersLibrarians.com

Library of Congress Cataloging-in-Publication Data is available upon request.
ISBN 978-0-593-43222-8 (trade) — ISBN 978-0-593-43223-5 (lib. bdg.)

Printed in the United States of America
10 9 8 7 6 5 4 3 2 1

This book has been officially leveled by using the F&P Text Level Gradient™ Leveling System.

llama llama
dance recital fun

based on the bestselling children's book series

by Anna Dewdney

Random House 🏠 New York

Llama Llama is happy.

He is watching Luna

Giraffe practice her

dance steps.

"That was great!"

Llama Llama says.

Luna has a recital soon.

She feels nervous.

"I have a tummy ache!"

Luna says.

Llama Llama and Nelly Gnu try to help Luna.

"I know you will be great, Luna," says Llama Llama.

But Luna is still nervous.

She needs fresh air

to calm down.

Llama Llama has an idea.

"You can practice for us!"

he says.

"I'll try," says Luna.

Luna puts on some music
to practice.

Oh no!

She still feels nervous.

Llama Llama knows how to
help Luna.

He invites her over to his house
to play.

He has a surprise for Luna.

"It's a dance machine!"

says Llama Llama.

Mama Llama tells Luna that it is just for fun.

"A few deep breaths help me feel calmer," says Mama Llama.

Luna takes some deep breaths.

Now she is calm and having fun.

"Go, Luna!" calls Nelly Gnu.

The next day, everyone gathers for the dance recital.

"I hope Luna is not so nervous anymore," says Llama Llama.

"You and Nelly are such good friends for trying to help her," says Mama Llama.

"I'm sure she's going to be fine," she says.

"Welcome to our dance recital!"

says Zelda Zebra.

The dancers begin to perform.

Oh no!

Luna is missing.

Llama Llama and

Nelly Gnu help look

for her.

Nelly Gnu searches the school halls.

Llama Llama searches

the classrooms.

"Luna, where are you?"

asks Llama Llama.

There she is!

Luna is outside.

Luna is still too nervous to perform onstage.

"I can't dance with everyone watching me," she says.

Llama Llama helps Luna.

"We're excited to see you dance,"

Llama Llama says.

Luna takes a few deep breaths.

"I'm going to try," Luna says.

"The show must go on!"

The friends race back inside.

Nelly Gnu reminds Luna

how much fun they had

on the dance machine.

"Just dance and try to have fun," says Llama Llama.

Llama Llama has an idea!

He brings the dance machine

to the stage.

"Put your hands together for

Luna Giraffe and Friends!"

First, Llama Llama dances

onstage.

Then more friends come up

to dance!

Now it is Luna's turn.

She takes a deep breath and

dances perfectly!

Everyone cheers.

Luna is so happy.

She is lucky to have

such great friends.

Mama Llama is proud of
Llama Llama for helping Luna.
They celebrate in the best
possible way—

with ice cream and
a dance party!